"See, guys?"

said Jimmy, leaning against the fireplace. "It's just a plain old house. And there's nothing in here to be scared of."

Suddenly a cold breeze whipped through the room. A moment later, the kids heard a voice—a strange, whispering voice. "You are wrong, little man. There is plenty to be scared of."

"Who said that?" asked Jimmy as he squeezed up close to the other Clues Kids.

"Get out . . ." the mysterious voice rose. "Get out while you can."

From somewhere in the house the kids heard a door slam. A second later they heard footsteps coming closer and closer.

"It's him," Lee shouted. "The ghost of Shockly Manor! And he's coming for us!"

The Ghost of Shockly Manor

•

William Alexander

•

Troll Associates

Cover art: Judith Sutton
Illustrated by: Dave Henderson

Library of Congress Cataloging-in-Publication Data

Alexander, William, (date)
    The ghost of Shockly Manor / William Alexander.
        p.   cm.—(The Clues Kids; #2)
    Summary: The Clues Kids try to find out whether there really is a
ghost in the spooky house known as Shockly Manor.
        ISBN 0-8167-1694-3 (lib. bdg.)   ISBN 0-8167-1695-1 (pbk.)
    [1. Mystery and detective stories.   2. Foster home care—Fiction.]
I. Title. II. Series: Alexander, William.   The Clues Kids; #2.
PZ7.A3786Gh 1990
[Fic]—dc20   89-36544

A TROLL BOOK, published by Troll Associates,
Mahwah, NJ 07430

Copyright © 1990 by Troll Associates, Mahwah, New Jersey

Printed in the United States of America.

10   9   8   7   6   5   4   3   2   1

JAY LOCKE

<u>Code name:</u> Clicker—Jay takes the pictures...lots of pictures. No clue escapes his lens because he shoots everything—windows, pets, doorknobs, lint—everything.

T.J. BOOKER

<u>Code name:</u> Smoke Screen—T.J. is the greatest disguise artist in the world (he asked me to say that). Actually, he does make up some great disguises. Some of them are pretty strange...but that's T.J.

JIMMY LOCKE

<u>Code name:</u> Jaws—He's the information man. He asks the questions. With his razor-sharp mind (he made me say that), Jimmy can break down any suspect.

DOTTIE BREWSTER

<u>Code name:</u> Short Stuff—She's the normal one of the bunch. Dottie looks for clues, tails crooks, keeps track of their fees, and tries to keep the others out of trouble. That's harder than you think!

LEE VAN THO

<u>Code name:</u> Smudge—Lee gets the fingerprints. He really gets the fingerprints. He usually makes a mess getting the prints, but he gets them!

C·H·A·P·T·E·R
1

*T*his is the town of Dozerville, Illinois, population 12,533 and a half. The half is an honorary citizenship given to a pet chimp named Boswell.

Though he can't vote in any elections, Boswell does attend some of the town meetings. He likes the snacks they serve—especially the banana bread.

Things are pretty normal in Dozerville.

On Webb Avenue Officer Anton Novak walks his beat.

He knows this town well. He can feel its pulse, hear its whispered secrets—smell its pepperoni. With twenty-six pizza parlors in town, *anyone* can smell the pepperoni.

And there are a dozen tales this police officer could tell. But this isn't *his* story.

This is the story of five foster children who live on Webb Avenue. Five junior crime fighters who call themselves the Clues Kids.

"This is going to be the best birthday party we've ever given!" said ten-year-old T.J. Booker.

He sat on the kitchen counter, twirling his long, bushy moustache.

"It's the *only* party we've ever given!" said Dottie Brewster. "And take that stupid thing off."

"It's not stupid," T.J. grumbled. "What does an eight-year-old girl know, anyway?"

Dottie jumped from her chair and placed her hands on her hips. "I know it's a dumb disguise. No normal person has an *orange* moustache."

"Oh." T.J. looked embarrassed as he pulled the fake moustache from his lip. The bright orange color had been quite a contrast to his dark brown skin. "I got it for my Halloween costume," T.J. explained. "Wait'll you see it. Boy, will you be surprised."

"I just hope we can surprise the Chief," said a dark-haired Vietnamese boy.

Lee Van Tho popped a handful of chocolate-covered raisins into his mouth. "We've been trying to keep his birthday party a secret for a week now."

"Don't worry, Lee." Twelve-year-old Jay Locke ran his fingers through his sandy brown hair. "Everything will be fine. The Chief doesn't suspect a thing."

"Not yet," said Lee. "But there's still a lot we have to do. How are we going to remember it all?"

Jimmy, Jay's twin brother, looked up from his notepad. "That's no problem," he said. "I'm making a list of all our assignments."

Just then Mrs. Patty Klink came rushing into the kitchen, loaded down with cookbooks. She

was a small woman in her fifties, with red hair and bright blue eyes.

"I'm glad you're making a list, Jimmy," she said, dropping the books on the table. "Saturday is only four days off. And there are still a million things to do."

T.J. leaned back against the counter. "It must be weird to have a birthday on Halloween."

"Yeah," said Lee. "Doesn't the Chief worry about ghosts or witches wrecking his birthday?"

Patty Klink smiled. "It hasn't bothered Phil in all the years I've known him. And I doubt it will this year."

Patty and Phil Klink were the kids' foster parents. Over a year ago they'd brought these five children home from the county shelter. Each child had come with special needs and problems, but the Klinks had shown them all love and tenderness. And, after a while, the children had come to think of the Klinks—and each other—as family.

"But Phil *will* be upset if I don't pick up his present before the party," Mrs. Klink continued. "I've been attending so many community affairs meetings lately, I've hardly had time to do anything else."

"Who's coming to the party?" Jay asked.

Patty Klink paused for a moment, looking very puzzled. "Oh, my," she said slowly. "I haven't finished sending out the invitations."

"Why don't you do that now," Jimmy suggested. "Meanwhile, we'll finish working on our list."

"All right," said Mrs. Klink. "That will be a

great help to me." She grabbed her address book from her purse and hurried off to the den.

"You know, Mrs. Klink isn't the only one with a problem," said Jay. "We have one too."

"What is it?" Dottie asked.

Jay flopped into a chair. "We don't have a present for the Chief."

"That's right," said Jimmy.

"That's because we don't have enough money." Lee sighed. "It's hard to buy a terrific gift with only eight dollars."

"Eight dollars and fifty-six cents," Dottie corrected him.

"So what do we do?" Jay asked.

Jimmy leaned back in his chair and smiled. "No problem," he said. "I've got it all worked out."

"You mean you know what we can buy the Chief?" asked Dottie.

"No," Jimmy replied smugly. "But I've fixed it so we'll have enough money to buy him whatever we want."

A worried expression appeared on T.J.'s face. "How?" he asked.

Jimmy pulled a sheet of paper from his notebook. "I got Mr. Letterman to print these," he said.

"What is it?" asked Jay.

"A flyer," Jimmy replied. "And it says, 'We won't feed your parrot. We won't pet your frog. But boy, are we great at walking your dog. For the best dog walkers in town call—' "

"Dog walkers!" Lee shouted. He grabbed the paper out of Jimmy's hand and read it. "You advertised us as dog walkers?"

"Sure," Jimmy said with a big smile. "We'll charge fifty cents a dog. We'll have a business, make lots of money, and Dottie can be the treasurer."

Dottie took the flyer from Lee. "Did you put these up already?"

"All around the school," Jimmy replied, checking his notes. "Plus the laundromat on Washington Street and the supermarket on Buyer Avenue. When people read this ad, the phone will start ringing like crazy."

Just then the front doorbell rang.

Jimmy shrugged his shoulders. "Guess our first customer decided to walk over." He got up from the table and went to answer the door.

Lee stared after Jimmy for a moment. Then he turned toward the other kids. "Do you suppose that this time one of Jimmy's ideas might really work?" he asked.

Before anyone could answer, they heard Jimmy call out from the front of the house. "Sure we can do it," he said with enthusiasm. "We're the best dog walkers in town."

"So he got one customer," said T.J. "That doesn't mean anything."

"Come on in—folks," Jimmy called out again.

"Folks?" the kids exclaimed.

A second later, Jimmy poked his head into the kitchen. "Come on, you guys. We've got three customers waiting in the living room!" With that, he was gone.

"Three customers," said Jay. "We can handle three customers."

The phone rang.

"I bet that's not the Avon Lady," said T.J. as he picked up the receiver.

Dottie got up from her chair and started for the living room. "I don't know why," she said. "But I've got a bad feeling about this."

Lee shrugged his shoulders. "Gee, guys—it's only a few little dogs. How bad could it be?"

The following afternoon, Lee found out.

He was practically running through one of Dozerville's wealthiest districts, Creston Hills. All around him were large, glamorous homes with freshly cut lawns and perfectly trimmed hedges.

But Lee wasn't enjoying any of it. He was being dragged along the street by his first assignment—four terriers, a sheepdog, and a St. Bernard.

He was not happy.

"Slow down, you guys," Lee called out. "What are you trying to do—pull my arm off?"

But the dogs didn't seem to hear him. Lee pulled on their leashes, trying to slow them down. But they kept right on barking, sniffing, running, and pulling. It was all Lee could do to keep up.

Overhead, the October skies were dark with rain clouds. And Lee could hear the threatening sound of thunder rumbling in the distance.

"Oh, great," Lee mumbled to himself. "That's all I need. To get stuck with six wet, smelly dogs."

As he reached the top of a hill, Lee's thoughts changed drastically—from the cheery picture of stuffing Jimmy's mouth with old socks straight to fear. Halloween-type fear.

In front of Lee stood one of the strangest old houses he had ever seen.

The mansion was four stories tall and painted a dull gray. Its shutters were a deep, dark green, almost black. A large, shabby lawn surrounded the house, and a tall, black iron fence ran across the front of the property. The front gate swung loosely back and forth, its rusty hinges creaking in the wind. And the whole house looked lost and alone.

Lee could just read the weathered, fancy sign hanging from the metal arch over the gate.

"Shockly Manor," he said in a soft whisper. "That's the place where that old inventor died."

The house reminded him of every horror film he had ever seen. And all he wanted to do was leave.

But just as he started to turn away, something caught his eye. A strange, yellowish glow appeared in one of the first-floor windows.

That's weird, Lee thought. *The place is supposed to be empty.*

Suddenly, the dogs went wild. They began barking and howling. Then the terriers started pulling him toward the house.

"Take it easy, you guys," Lee shouted. In his mind a terrible thought began to form. "This is just like the movie I saw last week. *Revenge of the Vampire Fruit Bat!*"

Lee pulled on the leashes, trying to turn the dogs away from the house.

As he struggled with the dogs, he looked up at the old mansion once more. That was when he saw it. The yellowish glow was a face—a thin, glowing face with hollow eyes, like a skull.

Lee found he had the strength of ten flowing through his body. And the dogs had to run to keep up with him.

Only one word came from his mouth as he made his way down the hill. But it came out loud and often. "Ghost!" Lee screamed as the thunder rumbled overhead. "Ghost!"

C·H·A·P·T·E·R
2

"**I**'m telling you, I saw what I see—saw!" Lee paced back and forth in front of the living room couch. His arms waved wildly in the air, and his voice hit its highest pitch.

"There are ghosts at Shockly Manor!" he shouted. "Ghosts—and who knows what else."

"Take it easy, Lee," Jay urged his brother. He and the other kids were sprawled across the living room furniture like rag dolls.

Their afternoon had been no picnic. Each had discovered that dog walking was for the birds. They were glad they only had one dog, Snoop, in their family.

"All you saw was a curtain waving in the breeze," Jimmy mumbled. He was lying on the floor with a pillow over his face.

Lee dropped down next to him. "A curtain doesn't have eyes, wise guy!" He yanked the pillow up. "You ever see a curtain with eyes?"

"No," Jimmy quickly replied. "And I've never seen a glowing ghost, either."

"Look, Lee," said Jay. "You were tired from walking the dogs. Maybe you just imagined it."

"We're all tired," Dottie said quietly. She sat

with her teddy bear, curled up in the Chief's overstuffed chair.

"Tired?" T.J. exclaimed. "I had to walk three different sets of dogs," he said. "I'm *dead* tired."

Lee's eyes flashed. "Don't say that!"

"It's just a figure of speech," T.J. replied.

"Look, Lee," said Jimmy, pushing himself up on his elbows. "Everybody knows there are no such things as ghosts. Right, guys?"

No one answered.

Jimmy rolled his eyes. "Hmmm . . . looks like maybe *everybody* doesn't know it."

"If there are no ghosts," said Lee, "then how come there are so many ghost stories? Even Cosmic Cop is after a ghost this week."

"Cosmic has a ghost story because it's the week before Halloween!" Jimmy grumbled. "And he's after Telstar Toombs, a vampire—not a ghost!"

"Oh, that makes it a lot better," Lee replied.

"I'd rather fight a ghost than a vampire any day." T.J. picked up his glass of milk and took a long sip.

"Come on," said Jimmy. "You don't really believe in this stuff." He turned from one child to another. "Jay, T.J., Dottie?"

T.J. shrugged his shoulders.

"I don't know," said Jay. "There are ghost stories in every country and language. That's pretty hard to ignore."

Jimmy had turned to Dottie, to see what she had to say, when he noticed that she was trembling.

"What's the matter, Dottie?" he asked.

Dottie pulled her teddy bear as close as she

could. "I was thinking about the children's shelter." Her voice wasn't much more than a whisper. "I was afraid to sleep in the dark, even though there were other girls in the room."

"What were you afraid of?" asked Jimmy.

"Monsters," she said softly. "I used to call them Shadow Things. I was afraid they'd come and take me away . . . forever."

"How did you ever get any sleep?" Lee asked.

Dottie held up her teddy bear. "Benny Boo took care of me. One of the older kids gave him to me as a good-bye present when she left."

"The shelter was pretty scary for all of us," said T.J. "But now the only spooky thing I want to see is the next episode of *Cosmic Cop*." He jumped off the couch and turned on the TV and the VCR. "Yesterday, he got trapped in a haunted asteroid."

"I'm glad the Chief taped it for us," said Jimmy.

Within seconds the voice of their cartoon hero boomed from the TV speakers. "The only thing that will stop Telstar Toombs," said Cosmic Cop, "is a silver carrot. Or is it a bottle of pink lemonade? I can never remember which."

Lee looked away from the TV set. "But what about the ghost at Shockly Manor?" he pleaded.

"I think you got a bad Bozo Burger from Clownie's," Jimmy said with a smile. Clownie's was Lee's favorite hamburger place. "Now, let's just drop it and watch the show."

Lee sat quietly and watched the episode with the other kids. But in the back of his mind, the Shockly Manor ghost was far from a *dead* issue.

He shivered a little. Well, it was *far* from being dropped.

Wrighter Elementary School was the oldest school in Dozerville. The staff was proud of its library, and its up-to-date teaching methods. The school board even boasted, "Anything children want to know, they can learn here."

Lee put that boast to the test.

He spent most of the following day asking everyone at the school about Shockly Manor.

When three o'clock rolled around, Lee had gathered quite a bit of information. And he wasn't the only one. The other kids had been asking around, too.

"Mr. Whaler told me that Old Man Shockly was some kind of inventor," Jay said with enthusiasm. He and the other kids had gathered at their usual spot—a low stone wall at the edge of the school grounds.

"Not just any old inventor," said Dottie. "He was a genius. And he became rich from his inventions."

"So what does that have to do with ghosts?" Jimmy asked sarcastically.

Lee lowered his voice. "People say there have been a lot of weird things going on at the manor."

"Like what?" Jay asked.

"Like strange noises," Lee replied. "And shadowy figures sneaking around the house. There've even been a few burglaries."

Jay shook his head. "What jerk would rob an empty old house?"

"Not the manor, dummy," Lee shouted, then

suddenly lowered his voice again. "There've been a lot of burglaries in the neighborhood."

"That makes sense," said Dottie. "Mrs. Klink says that Creston Hills is one of the nicest neighborhoods in Dozerville. The houses cost a lot."

"Yeah," said T.J. "You need to have tons of money, or be friends with the president of the United States."

"If there's a burglar in Creston Hills," Jay said thoughtfully, "then maybe we have our next case."

Jimmy's eyes widened. "You're right. The Dozerville police could surely use my—I mean, our ace detecting skills."

"Oh, brother." Dottie sighed.

"So how do we start?" asked T.J.

"We start by finding out all we can about the neighborhood," said Jay.

"Sure," said Jimmy. "We don't have to walk any dogs until about five o'clock."

"I bet Mr. P.T. Landis could tell us anything we wanted to know," said Lee.

Jimmy raised an eyebrow. "Who is Mr. P.T. Landis?"

"The real-estate agent for Creston Hills." Lee tried to sound very smug as he pronounced the words. "He's also the man who's taking care of Shockly Manor."

Jimmy threw his hands up in the air. "You won't give up on this ghost thing, will you?"

Lee stuck out his chest. "Not until I prove I *seen* what I saw. Uh, *saw* what I seen, uh . . . oh, skip it. Let's go."

The offices of P.T. Landis were located on

Field Avenue, the street where the Creston Hills district began.

The kids were impressed the moment they entered the building. All the furniture was made from light-colored wood and soft, shiny leather. And the walls were lined with photos and diagrams of Creston Hills' most beautiful homes.

Although the offices were large, the kids saw only two people working there—a short man with a bald spot on his head, and a lady with very long hair. Both people were dressed as if they were posing for a clothing ad.

"May I help you?" the woman asked as they approached her desk.

"Yes, please," said Jimmy. "We'd like to see Mr. Landis."

The man smiled and extended his right hand. "I'm P.T. Landis. Landis is my name—land *is* my game." He shook hands with everyone. "This is my secretary, Miss Acres." The well-dressed lady gave them a faint grin, then rose and went over to a set of file cabinets.

"Now, what can I sell you?" Mr. Landis teased. "A town house, a manor, or maybe a rolling estate?"

"Actually," Jimmy replied, "we've come about the burglaries in the Creston Hills area."

"And about Shockly Manor," Lee added.

The smile faded from Mr. Landis's lips. "Kids," he said, clearing his throat, "the people around here don't like to talk about the robberies, or Shockly Manor. What makes you so curious about them?"

Jimmy pulled out his notepad. "We want to know about the—"

"The weird noises coming from the manor," Lee interrupted.

"Right," said Jimmy. He looked annoyed. "We've also heard stories about robberies. And—"

Lee leaned past him. "And about the shadowy figures seen around the manor."

Jimmy gave Lee a dirty look. "Now people say that the burglar is never seen—"

"Neither are ghosts," Lee added.

Jimmy threw up his hands. "Will you quit jumping in!" he shouted.

"I know I saw something at the manor!" Lee yelled back.

Jay and T.J. tried to calm them down.

"Please excuse my brothers, sir," said Dottie as she walked up to Mr. Landis.

"Your—brothers?" Mr. Landis seemed puzzled.

"That's us," T.J. said with a smile. "We live with the Klinks. You know—Mr. Klink used to be the chief of police."

"Oh." Mr. Landis still looked confused.

"It's a long story," said Dottie. "Anyway, my brother Lee was at the manor yesterday. And—he thought he saw a ghost."

"I *did*," Lee insisted.

"So we were wondering," Jay put in, "if you could tell us anything about the house, or Mr. Shockly . . ."

"Or the robberies," Jimmy grumbled.

Mr. Landis rose from the desk and walked around the kids. At last, he turned to Lee. "I can tell you one thing. Stay away from the manor."

"I didn't go in or break anything," Lee said quickly.

"That's not what I mean." Mr. Landis rubbed his bald spot. "Mr. Thomas E. Shockly was a genius. He could invent anything."

"We know that," Jimmy responded.

"Maybe you do. But you don't know what happened after he died." The kids all moved in closer. "They found a note attached to his will. And in it, Mr. Thomas E. Shockly swore that he would find a way to return from the beyond."

"You're kidding," T.J. said breathlessly.

The real-estate agent frowned. "I wish I were. Mr. Shockly made sure I couldn't sell the house for a whole year. That's when he planned to return—one year from the day he passed away. That deadline—"

"Don't say that," Lee whispered.

"That *date* was one week ago," Mr. Landis continued.

The kids were silent for a moment. All of them had a million thoughts racing through their brains. But it was Lee who finally spoke up.

"Now you guys *have* to believe me," he said with a quaver in his voice. "I thought I saw something yesterday. And now I'm sure of it. Mr. Shockly has kept his word." Lee pointed to a calendar on the desk. "It's Halloween . . . and *he's* come home."

C·H·A·P·T·E·R
3

"*I*f Old Man Shockly has come back from the grave," said Jimmy, "then I'm a monkey's uncle!"

"Great," Lee snapped back. "I'll buy you some bananas."

"Look, children," said Mr. Landis. "I'm not saying there's a ghost in the manor. But there *have* been some strange things going on there. It's best if you keep as far away as possible. Just to be—safe."

"Don't worry," Lee said quickly. "I just made *safe* my middle name."

"Good," Mr. Landis replied. "Now if you'll excuse me, I have a lot of work to do."

"Don't let us stop you, Mr. Landis," said Jimmy, trying to sound very professional. "I know what it's like to be busy. I'm pretty busy, too, with my—"

Jay tapped his brother on the shoulder. "Say good-bye, Jimmy."

"Good-bye, Mr. Landis." Jimmy shook the real-estate agent's hand. "It's been a rare pleasure *converting* with you. Uh ... I mean conversing."

Dottie shook her head as she turned toward the front door. "Oh, brother."

Five minutes later, the kids were walking along Penny Lane, the main street in the Creston Hills area.

"I still think this is a bad idea," said Lee. "Why do we have to go near that house?"

"Because we didn't learn anything about the robberies from Mr. Landis." Jimmy sounded annoyed. "So the next thing an ace detective does is look over the crime scene. You know, the lay of the land. Snoop around, dig in the—"

"We got it," the kids said in unison.

"I'm kind of curious about the manor, anyway," said Jay as they crossed LaCrosse Avenue.

"Me, too," said T.J. "I've never seen a real haunted house before."

"It's not haunted," Jimmy insisted. "And after you see this place, you'll know I'm right."

"Don't bet on it, wise guy," Lee said nervously. "Don't bet on it."

Within a few minutes the kids were standing in front of the black iron gates of Shockly Manor.

From the moment they reached the house, everything looked different. It seemed as if the gray autumn skies turned darker. And the chill in the air felt sharper—almost biting.

T.J. let out a low whistle as he stared through the fence. "You were wrong, Jimmy. This place is even spookier than Lee said."

Dottie felt a small shiver run down her back.

"Let's ask some of the neighbors about this place," Jay suggested. He pulled out his camera and took a few pictures, catching the house, the sign over the gate—and the back of Jimmy's head. Accidents happen.

"Good idea," said Jimmy eagerly. He reached into his schoolbag and pulled out his notepad. "That way we can ask about the robberies, too."

There were houses on either side of Shockly Manor. The one on the left looked almost as old. It was painted beige, with dark brown shutters, and there was a large, beautiful flower garden in front.

The other house was a little different. It was lemon yellow, with bright red shutters. And there were statues on the front lawn—five large, pink flamingos.

"Let's start at *that* house," Jay said. "I've got to see who lives there."

"Okay," said Jimmy. "But you'd better let me do the questioning this time." He shot Lee a dirty look. "I know how to get people to talk."

Maybe Jimmy knew how to get people to talk—but he wasn't any good at getting them to stop.

The occupants of the yellow house were Grace and William Grossip. They were fairly wealthy people, both in their fifties. Mr. Grossip wore an emerald-green lounging jacket with large, satin lapels. And he had fancy-looking rings on every finger.

Mrs. Grossip was a large woman with shiny silver hair. She wore a long dress with flowers printed on it. Lots and lots of flowers.

She was also covered in jewels.

"These people could open a jewelry store," T.J. whispered to Dottie. She quickly poked him with her elbow.

After the kids introduced themselves, the Grossips led them into a very fancy living room. There was a high marble fireplace on one side of the room. And above it was a large painting of a man with a guitar. Jay thought he looked like an old rock-and-roll singer. But he couldn't remember his name.

Once they were all seated, Jimmy claimed that he and the kids were working on a school assignment about Creston Hills. That was about all he got to say.

"There used to be twenty-two elm trees on this street," Mr. Grossip offered.

"That's nice," said Jimmy. "But—"

"Twenty-four," said Mrs. Grossip pleasantly.

"That's nice," said Jimmy. "Now I—"

"I remember it well," Mrs. Grossip continued. "They planted the last one on the day we moved in."

"That's nice, ma'am." Jimmy looked at the other kids. He was asking them for help.

But they didn't say a word. They just smiled at him.

Mr. Grossip poked at the fire in the fireplace. "It was a fine neighborhood then. Not like it is now."

"What do you—" Jimmy never finished his question.

"Not with all the robberies," said Mr. Grossip. "A neighbor of ours was robbed just last night."

Jimmy tried again. "Did they see the—"

"And then there are the strange goings-on at Shockly Manor," Mrs. Grossip went on.

Jimmy realized that one word was all he'd have a chance to say. "Strange?"

"Oh, yes," Mrs. Grossip replied. "Strange noises in the night—"

"And strange people always coming and going," Mr. Grossip added.

"People?" said Jimmy, getting in another key word.

"Yes," Mr. Grossip replied. "A man—"

"Two men, dear," said Mrs. Grossip, raising her fingers. "Tall, thin, and dressed in black suits."

"Oh, yes." Mr. Grossip nodded his head. "They always come in the evenings."

Lee looked out the large picture window at the old manor next door. From this side, the tall, second-floor windows looked like hollow eyes. And the porch railing looked like—teeth. Together, they made Shockly Manor appear to be grinning at him. Lee swallowed hard, then turned away.

"Things have surely changed." Mr. Grossip sighed heavily. He looked up at the painting of the singer. "It's not like it was in nineteen fifty-five—"

"Fifty-six, dear. That was when . . ."

It took the kids twenty minutes to get out of the Grossips' home. During that time they'd learned about the neighborhood and Shockly Manor. They'd also learned about elm trees, Fifties music, and the rising cost of pink flamingos.

"I didn't think anybody could outtalk Jimmy," said T.J. as they stood in front of the second house.

"Thanks a lot," Jimmy grumbled.

"I'm *so* glad we let you do the questioning," Dottie teased. "See how much we learned?"

"We learned not to go near Shockly Manor," said Lee.

"What about Shockly Manor?" said a voice from behind them.

The kids turned to see a thin, stern-faced woman standing only a few feet behind them.

"Where'd she come from?" Lee whispered to Jay.

"I don't know," Jay replied. "I didn't even hear her footsteps."

The lady had wild, frizzy hair and long, painted fingernails. She wore a fur coat that hung down to her suede boots.

Her teeth were large and very white, and her voice was low and raspy-sounding. But it was her eyes that really bothered the kids. They were shaped like leaves, light in color, bright, and quick-moving—like the eyes of an animal.

She stepped closer to the children. "I said, what about Shockly Manor?"

"Nothing special," said Jimmy. He tried to smile, but the lady's eyes made him nervous. "We were just wondering about it—you know, curious."

"Who are you?" the woman asked suspiciously. "I've never seen you around here before."

Jimmy cleared his throat. "We're the—"

Jay quickly interrupted his brother. "We walk dogs around here, Miss—Miss, uh?"

"Meely," she said, her white teeth flashing. "Miss Elsa Meely. I live here." She pointed to the beige-colored house.

"Dogs, eh?" Miss Meely slowly turned toward

30

Lee, and her eyes narrowed. "Yes . . . I saw this little man with several dogs, just the other day. He was screaming at the top of his lungs."

Lee took a step behind Jimmy and Jay. "That's because I saw a ghost in the window of Shockly Manor."

"He *thought* he saw a ghost, Miss Meely," said Jimmy. "I've been trying to tell him that nobody really believes in them."

"I do." Miss Meely's eyes grew wide, and a wicked grin appeared on her face. "And I suggest you stay away from Shockly Manor. The ghost of Thomas Shockly has returned. And I'm sure anyone who enters that house won't like what they find."

Miss Meely started up the path to her home, then stopped. "Remember what I've said, children. Stay away from Shockly Manor."

Miss Meely pulled her fur coat tightly around her and marched into her house.

"That does it," shouted Lee. "Mr. Landis and the Grossips say there are weird things going on in the manor. And a lady who looks like a wolf says stay away from it."

Lee took a deep breath. "There's only one thing we should do—"

"Right," said Jimmy. "Go into that house and look around."

"Uh-uh," said Lee, shaking his head and backing away from the kids. "The only way I'm going in there is if you carry me."

"Put me down," Lee demanded as the other boys carried him through the front door of the manor.

——•——

31

Once inside, they carefully dropped him on the polished wood floor.

"It sure was dumb of them to leave the gate open and the door unlocked," said Jay.

Lee got to his feet and looked around. "It was dumber of us to come in here!"

"Wow," said Jay. He pulled out his camera and started clicking away. "This room is twice as big as our living room."

"And this is just the front hall." Dottie took hold of Jay's jacket. "A very dark front hall."

The room was gray and gloomy-looking. Very little light filtered in through the open door and the shuttered windows. The kids could just make out the high ceiling and the old paintings on the walls.

Ahead of them a winding staircase led up to the next floor. And on either side of them a dark corridor led to some other part of the house.

"Where do you think that one goes?" asked Jimmy, pointing to the hallway on the left.

"Let's find out," said Jay.

"Let's go home," Lee said nervously.

The boys ignored Lee and headed for the corridor. Dottie followed, still holding on to Jay's jacket.

Halfway down the corridor, Dottie stepped on something. "Wait a minute," she said.

She picked up the tiny object. "It's a pearl earring," she said, holding it up for everyone to see.

"It probably belonged to Mrs. Shockly," said Jimmy. "Keep it. We'll give it to Mr. Landis the next time we see him. Now, come on."

The corridor opened up into a large room filled with old furniture.

"This must be the living room," said Jimmy. "Boy, does it smell funny in here."

T.J. gave him a nudge. "You'd smell funny, too, if you hadn't been cleaned in a year."

The kids moved into the room and stopped next to a huge, dark fireplace.

"See, guys?" said Jimmy, leaning against the fireplace. "It's just a plain old house. And there's nothing in here to be scared of."

Suddenly a cold breeze whipped through the room. A moment later, the kids heard a voice—a strange, whispered voice. "You are wrong, little man. There is plenty to be scared of."

"Who said that?" asked Jimmy as he squeezed closer to the others.

"Get out." The mysterious voice rose. "Get out while you can."

From somewhere in the house the kids heard a door slam. A second later, they heard footsteps coming closer and closer.

"It's him," Lee shouted. "The ghost of Shockly Manor! And he's coming for us!"

C·H·A·P·T·E·R
4

"***R***un!" Lee screamed as a maniacal laugh echoed through the room.

The other kids really didn't need his advice. With Jimmy in the lead, they were already racing through the door and down the narrow hallway.

"Head for the front door," Jimmy shouted.

With freedom almost in sight, the kids burst into the front hall—and slammed into something. When they looked up, they were facing two tall men dressed in black suits. The men stood between the kids and the front door—the *closed* front door.

"You guys aren't from the phone company, are you?" said T.J., trying to be funny.

The two men looked at each other, then at the children, and smiled.

"My name is Mr. Casper," said the man with long, blond hair. There was a touch of an accent in his speech. "And this is my associate, Mr. Coombs."

"Coombs," Lee whispered. "That sounds like Toombs—the vampire in *Cosmic Cop*."

The dark-skinned man bowed slightly. "We

are here to meet Mr. Landis, the realtor," said Mr. Coombs. His voice was very soft and silky. Lee could feel the hair stand up on the back of his neck.

"May we ask why you are here?" said Mr. Casper.

"We were just looking for our—dog," said Jimmy, thinking quickly. He and Jay began to nudge the other kids around the two men, and toward the front door.

"We have this great basset hound named Snoop," Jimmy went on.

"Yeah," said Jay. "He's a great dog, but he's always getting into strange places."

"Not that this place is strange," T.J. said quickly. "I mean, it's probably a great place."

The kids were almost at the door.

"Yeah," said Lee, reaching for the doorknob. "It's probably the greatest place in town."

"Well, we've got to go—now," said Jimmy.

Quickly, Lee yanked open the door and dashed outside. The other kids were right behind him.

"What about your dog?" Mr. Casper called out.

"If you see him," Jimmy yelled back, "tell him to call home!"

The kids raced across the lawn and through the iron gates. But they stopped suddenly when they reached the sidewalk.

"What's this?" Lee asked, breathing heavily. He carefully approached a long black car parked at the curb.

"It looks like a limousine," said Dottie. She was standing very close to Jay, staring at the car.

T.J. swallowed hard. "It also looks like a hearse."

"H—h—hearse?" Lee whispered.

Just then a clap of thunder boomed overhead.

Jimmy began to slowly back away from the car and the manor. "I think I hear Mrs. Klink calling us," he said with a tremor in his voice. "Let's go home."

As the kids tore off down the street, the door to Shockly Manor closed—very slowly.

The Klinks' old-fashioned house felt especially warm and comforting when the kids got home. They decided they wouldn't tell their foster parents about their adventure at Shockly Manor. After all, why worry them? Besides, they didn't want the Chief to interfere with their case.

But keeping the Chief in the dark was proving to be a little difficult. He kept roaming around the house. He'd walk in and out of the kitchen, where Mrs. Klink was on the phone trying to make party plans.

Each time the Chief came into the room, Mrs. Klink had to disguise what she was saying.

"It will be a wonderful party—uh, *parting*!" Patty Klink said out loud. "The mayor's *parting* remarks were wonderful!"

"The Chief's in the kitchen again," said Dottie. "He'll be coming in here next."

"Well, just don't say anything about the party or Shockly Manor," Jimmy said anxiously. "We've got to keep walking people's dogs until—"

"Until what?" said Phil Klink, stepping into the room.

"Until we have enough money," said Jimmy.

The Chief raised an eyebrow. "*Extra* money?" he said pleasantly. "Isn't your allowance enough?"

"Uh-uh—" Jimmy stuttered. He couldn't think of a quick answer.

"We need to buy some—stuff," Dottie piped up. "You know, Cosmic Cop detective, uh—stuff."

"Oh," said the Chief. He sounded a little disappointed. "That's nice."

"Yeah," said T.J. "You never know when a crime wave will strike. We want to be ready for it."

"Crime wave, ha." Phil Klink grunted. "We have one of those right now. All those burglaries in the Creston Hills district. The boys at the station are having a tough time with that one."

Lee leaned toward the Chief. "Have they found any clues, or fingerprints?"

"Nope," said the Chief. He tucked his thumbs behind his suspenders. "Now if *I* were handling this, things would be different."

"Why don't you offer to help them out?" asked Dottie. "Maybe just for a few days."

Jimmy tried to hide a smile. He knew what Dottie was trying to do—keep the Chief busy for the next two days.

"Yeah," he said. "Tomorrow's Friday. That's the day you usually go visit the station house, anyway."

"I *could* go tomorrow," said the Chief. "But I don't know about Saturday. It's, uh, kind of special." Phil Klink looked up at the ceiling— for no particular reason. "You *do* know what Saturday is, don't you?" he asked.

"Sure we do," said Jay.

Phil Klink smiled.

"It's Halloween," Jay continued. "And boy, are we going to have fun trick-or-treating."

"Oh," said the Chief. "I see." He turned around and headed toward the kitchen.

"A large *part!*" yelled Mrs. Klink. "He had a big *part* in that movie! I'll call you later, Denise."

"That was close," said T.J. "Do you think he suspects?"

"Nah," said Jimmy. "I was too clever for him."

"Oh, brother." Dottie sighed.

"Look, guys," said Jay, pointing to a wall clock. "It's five-fifteen, and we've got dogs to walk."

"I'm not walking those dogs near that house again." Lee fell back against the couch pillows.

"You've got to," Jimmy insisted. "We promised our client."

Lee folded his arms across his chest. "I don't care. I'm not going anywhere near that house."

"What about the money we'll lose?" asked Jay. "We need that for the Chief's present. I even thought of a great one. Gold golf clubs."

Dottie shook her head. "The Chief doesn't play golf."

"Oh—that's right," Jay mumbled.

"I want to help," Lee pleaded, "but—well—"

"Don't worry about it, Lee." T.J. patted him on the back. "I'll handle it. It'll be a good chance for me to try out one of my new disguises. But you have to take my turn walking Snoop."

Lee nodded. "Okay."

"Great, then," said Jay. "Let's get going."

"Jay," Dottie said nervously. "Can I walk my dogs with you?"

"Sure thing," said Jay. He could tell something was bothering her, but he didn't ask what. "And we'll all meet back here at six o'clock."

As the kids passed the kitchen, they heard, "Partly! That's right, June. The day is *partly* over."

Only two more days, thought Dottie. *We can make it—I hope.*

At five-forty-five, a hobo in red sneakers was being pulled past the Grossips' house.

The hobo was wearing an old coat, baggy pants, and a beat-up hat. He even had dirt smeared all over his face.

T.J. Booker was impressed with his latest creation. But the dogs weren't. In fact, they were having more fun pulling him than they had Lee.

But as they approached the gates of Shockly Manor, the dogs stopped.

"Come on, you guys," T.J. said nervously. "It's raining, and I don't want to hang around here."

T.J. tried pulling them away from the gate, but the dogs wouldn't move. They kept sniffing the ground and staring at the house.

Again T.J. pulled at their leashes. "Let's go, dogs. There are things around here I don't want to meet."

Suddenly one of the terriers broke free. In an instant the furry little dog bolted through the gate and darted behind the manor.

"Stop, you dumb dog!" T.J. shouted. Quickly,

he tied the other dogs to the fence. "If I'm not back in two minutes, go for help."

T.J. ran across the lawn as fast as he could.

As he reached the side of the house, the rain began to pour.

"I don't believe this," T.J. mumbled as he crept toward the back of the house. "It's raining, it's getting dark, and where am I? Creeping around a haunted house—alone. This is not smart."

Suddenly T.J. heard three little barks.

"That's it," he said as he approached the corner of the house. "Make some noise so I can find you."

T.J. turned the corner and found himself facing a wall of hedges about six feet high. The hedges were like a thick black curtain—with cracks of moonlight bleeding through.

"Oh, great," T.J. said angrily. "Now I've got to find a way through the hedges to get to the backyard."

Three more barks came out of the darkness. Then, suddenly, a yelp, a whimper—and silence.

T.J. froze in his tracks. The harsh wind blew rain into his eyes, making it hard for him to see.

"It's not my dog," T.J. told himself. "I don't have to go look for it." He tried to take a step backwards, then he heard another whimper.

T.J. froze again. Then, slowly, he started forward along the hedges. "Boy, am I stupid," he muttered. "Here, dog. Here, poochie. Here—"

The words caught in his throat, and his heart hammered in his chest.

He was alone in a dark, spooky place, with a

storm raging overhead. And a hand had just grabbed him by the shoulder.

One thought raced across his mind. In the horror movies, this was usually a real bad time for the hero.

C·H·A·P·T·E·R
5

TJ. spun around and found himself facing Miss Elsa Meely. She was dressed in a shiny black raincoat with the collar turned up around her face. She also had T.J.'s missing dog tucked under her left arm.

"What are you doing here?" she asked.

"Just walking these dogs—honest!" T.J. replied. "This one got away from me."

A loud clap of thunder rolled overhead. T.J. could hear the dogs howling by the gate. Was it the storm, or something else?

"Here," said Miss Meely. She thrust the terrier into T.J.'s arms. "Go home. And keep your dogs away from this house."

"You've got it, lady," said T.J. He took a few steps back from her, turned, and ran toward the fence.

As he reached the gate, T.J. looked back. Miss Meely was standing on the front steps of the manor. Her wild hair was blowing in the wind.

"Stay away from Shockly Manor," she yelled as a bolt of lightning split the sky. "Stay away!"

That was it for T.J. Once again, the dogs had a very fast trip home.

In his warmest pajamas and thickest robe, T.J. sat curled up on his bed. His hands were wrapped around his Cosmic Cop mug. The mug was filled with hot chocolate, piled high with gobs of marshmallows.

Jimmy, Jay, Lee, and Dottie sprawled around the room, with their own warm drinks. All of them were listening to the end of T.J.'s tale.

"And there she was—standing on the steps of Shockly Manor—with the special effects crew working overtime." T.J. took a sip from his cup and licked the marshmallow from his lips. "I'm telling you guys, ghost or not, there's something weird going on at that house."

"I agree," said Jay. "And it's about time the Clues Kids found out what."

"Why?" asked Lee.

"Because that's what detectives do, dummy." Jimmy took a sip from his cup of hot cider.

"Detectives don't investigate ghosts," Lee replied.

"Well, *we* do," replied Jay. "If ghosts *are* haunting Shockly Manor, then we've got to warn people."

"I'm with you," Jimmy said eagerly. He grabbed a pencil and paper from T.J.'s desk. "Where do we start?"

Jay ran his fingers through his sandy brown hair. "I guess we start with Mr. Landis. There's probably a lot more he can tell us about the manor."

"And about those two guys we saw," said Jimmy. "Mr. Casper and Mr. Coombs."

"Okay," Jay continued. "Tomorrow, Jimmy and I—"

45

"Hey," T.J. interrupted. "If it's Clues Kids time, then use our code names."

During their first case, the kids had assigned themselves code names. They used these names whenever they were on an assignment. T.J. thought it kept the bad guys guessing. The others weren't so sure.

"Okay." Jay sighed. "Jaws and I will go see Mr. Landis. In the meantime, Short Stuff and Smudge," he said, pointing at Dottie and Lee, "will—"

Lee jumped up from the bed. "I'm not going into that house!"

"You don't have to," Jay said calmly.

Lee relaxed and sat back down on the bed. "Good."

"But," Jay continued, "I want you and Short Stuff to find out all you can about Miss Meely. Smoke Screen," Jay looked at T.J., "will keep an eye on the manor while you guys check out the neighbors."

"Oh, no." Lee buried his head in one of T.J.'s pillows.

Jay turned to Dottie. He'd noticed their little sister had been unusually quiet all evening. "Are you okay, Dottie?" he asked.

Dottie nodded yes.

"Will you go with Lee and T.J. tomorrow?" Jay asked.

"Sure," said Dottie. She looked down at her closed right fist.

When the boys went back to making plans, Dottie opened her hand. She was holding the pearl earring she'd found in the manor house.

If this belonged to Mrs. Shockly, thought

Dottie, *I should return it. But I sure don't want to go into that house again.* Dottie didn't know what to do.

Finally, she slipped the earring into her pants pocket, and said nothing about it.

Friday afternoon came quickly. The kids raced home from school, dropped off their books, and left. They only had one hour to handle their assignments before they had to walk the dogs.

On Field Avenue, Jay and Jimmy chained up their bikes and entered the offices of P.T. Landis.

His secretary was just putting on her coat as the boys approached her desk.

"May we see Mr. Landis?" Jay asked politely.

"I'm sorry," said Miss Acres. "Mr. Landis is in with clients at the moment. And I was just leaving."

"We'll wait, if you don't mind," said Jay. "It's about Shockly Manor."

Miss Acres suddenly seemed very interested. "I remember you two from yesterday," she said, pointing from Jay to Jimmy. "And I'll bet you're the children who were spotted running from the manor."

Jimmy wasn't sure how they should answer her. "Well, uh—"

"You know that the manor is private property," she said with a serious tone in her voice. "And I believe Mr. Landis warned you about going there."

"You're right, Miss," Jay said apologetically. "But we found out something. And now we've really got to talk to Mr. Landis about it. Please."

"All right," said Miss Acres, after a moment of thought. "You can wait here until his clients leave." The secretary picked up her purse and gloves from her desk. "But don't disturb him until then. Agreed?"

"Don't worry," said Jimmy. "We'll sit right here and be perfect little angels."

"Somehow, I doubt that," said Miss Acres. She smiled and walked out the front door.

For the first few minutes, the boys sat quietly. They looked around, noticing different things about the office. Especially the designs of some of the most beautiful homes in Creston Hills that Mr. Landis had hanging on the walls.

But after a while, they became restless.

"I wonder how much longer he's going to be," said Jimmy. "We've got to get home soon."

"One way to find out," said Jay. He got up from his chair and crept over to the office door.

Placing his ear against the door, Jay could just make out three voices coming from the other side.

The first voice sounded like Mr. Landis. "Well, that settles it," he said. "You can take possession as soon as the bank finishes the paperwork. Are you sure you gentlemen don't want any coffee?"

"No, thank you," came another voice. Jay thought he detected a foreign accent.

"We don't drink . . . coffee," said the third.

There was no mistaking that soft, silky tone. Jay knew who the clients were.

He quickly rushed to Jimmy's side. "It's Mr. Casper and Mr. Coombs," he whispered. "They're in there with Mr. Landis. And I think they've just bought Shockly Manor."

Jimmy looked surprised and puzzled. "Why would any normal person buy a haunted house?"

Jay looked back at the door to Mr. Landis's private office. "What makes you think Casper and Coombs are normal?"

"What do you mean?" asked Jimmy.

"I don't know," Jay replied. "But when they leave, I'm going to follow them."

"But—"

Before Jimmy could say another word, the door to Mr. Landis's office opened. The realty agent walked out shaking the hands of Mr. Casper and Mr. Coombs.

"I look forward to seeing you Monday morning," Mr. Landis said happily.

"Please make that Monday evening," Mr. Coombs said politely.

"Yes," said Mr. Casper. "We will be busy until then."

"Very well," Mr. Landis replied. "Monday evening it is."

"Till then . . . good-bye, Mr. Landis," said Mr. Casper.

As the two men turned to leave, they noticed the boys.

Casper and Coombs smiled, then departed.

"What can I do for you boys?" asked Mr. Landis.

"Uh, nothing for me," Jay replied. "Uh, uh, I've got to go see the dentist."

A sympathetic frown crossed Mr. Landis's face. "Do you have a toothache?"

"Uh, no. But why wait?" Jay waved good-bye and ran out the door.

"Mr. Landis," said Jimmy, clearing his throat.

"Those two men have been seen going in and out of Shockly Manor a lot."

"I'm not surprised," said the realtor. "They've just bought the place."

"But what are they going to do with it?"

"They say they're part of some kind of scientific club. The manor will be perfect for their meetings, or something."

"Why would anyone want to hold meetings in a haunted house?" asked Jimmy.

Mr. Landis seemed to become uncomfortable. "Look, I'm just glad to be rid of the place, haunted or not."

"Mr. Landis," said Jimmy, looking a little embarrassed. "We were in the manor yesterday."

"I told you not to go near—"

"I know, sir," Jimmy interrupted. "But while we were in there, we heard a strange voice warning us to leave."

"When?" asked Mr. Landis.

"Let's see," said Jimmy, checking his notes. "We went in, walked down the hallway, Dottie found the earring, we went into the living room—and that's when it happened."

When Jimmy looked up from his notepad, Mr. Landis had a worried expression on his face.

For a moment he didn't say anything. Then, "I warned you about that house," said Mr. Landis. "Now the ghost knows you. And once a ghost has marked you—your fate is sealed."

"But—"

Mr. Landis gently took Jimmy by the shoulders. "I suggest you get rid of anything that ties

you to that house. And do it before it's too late."

Meanwhile, Jay was pedaling like crazy along Ashbin Road, on the outskirts of town. He'd been following Casper and Coombs's limousine since it left Mr. Landis's office.

It had moved slowly, almost ominously, along the streets of Dozerville. That had made it easy to tail.

But once it left town, the sleek black car picked up speed. Only the sharp, winding curves kept Jay from losing the car altogether.

I wonder where it's going, he thought as the car turned onto Nevermore Lane.

Jay looked at his watch. "It's almost five o'clock," he mumbled. "It'll be dark soon, and I'll have to get back to—"

Jay brought his bike to a sudden stop. Up ahead, Casper and Coombs's limousine drove through the gates of what looked like private property. A high stone wall surrounded the place, and Jay couldn't see what was on the other side.

Quickly he rode his bike up to the wall, and made his way to the gate. When he looked through the bars, Jay could see the limousine move along a narrow road and disappear among the trees.

It was then that he noticed a large sign attached to the wall. A name was painted on it in large gold letters. RAVENSWOOD RESTING PLOTS.

Jay felt his blood run cold. His suspects had just disappeared into a cemetery.

C·H·A·P·T·E·R
6

Casper and Coombs have just entered a cemetery, thought Jay. The question is, am I going to follow?

Jay looked up at the cloudy evening sky. For the third day in a row, the weather had been miserable. There had been no sunshine, and there would be no bright, shiny moon.

The answer was clear. "Not on your life," Jay muttered to himself. He pulled out his camera, took a few shots, then rode off as fast as he could.

While Jimmy was learning he'd been tagged by a ghost, and Jay was trailing black cars to cemeteries, the rest of the team was roaming Creston Hills.

They had asked a number of people about Miss Meely. But they hadn't found out much more than they already knew.

Miss Elsa Meely was well-off, lived alone, and was a very cranky person.

The only really interesting bit of news was that she and Mr. Thomas E. Shockly had been friends.

"I can't imagine her being anybody's friend," said T.J. He was standing behind a tree just down the street from Miss Meely's house. "She's pretty weird-looking, you know."

"I wouldn't talk." Dottie gave T.J. a slow up-and-down stare. "You don't look that great, either."

"I'm not supposed to." T.J. sounded annoyed. "I'm in disguise. Smoke Screen is on the job."

T.J.'s idea of a disguise was one of Phil Klink's old sweat shirts, matching pants, and a white wig made out of large cotton balls. He'd topped off the outfit with a pair of very thick glasses.

T.J. adjusted his glasses and pulled up his pants. They were a bit large for him. "I figured an old man jogging wouldn't attract attention. Not in this neighborhood." He admired his outfit. "What do you think?"

"Don't ask," said Dottie. She and Lee left T.J. behind the tree and headed across the street to Miss Meely's.

"Tell me again," Lee said as they reached the front door. "Why are we going to see the wolf lady?"

"Because it's the best way to find out about her," said Dottie. She rang the doorbell, then stepped away from the door.

Lee noticed. "Why did you do that?" he asked.

"Just in case," said Dottie.

The front door opened slightly, and there stood Miss Meely.

Dottie thought she looked different. Her hair was in a bun on the top of her head, and she was wearing overalls and work gloves.

Somehow, she didn't look as wild.

But in spite of her looks, she wasn't any nicer. "What do you children want now?" she asked.

Dottie had her story ready. "We wanted to apologize for bothering you yesterday."

"Fine," Miss Meely replied. "Apology accepted." She turned her gaze on Lee. "I hope you haven't brought any dogs with you."

"Uh, no—ma'am," Lee stuttered. "Not this time."

Lee had also noticed how different Miss Meely looked. But he'd noticed something else, too. On the floor, just inside the doorway, he could see a pile of wooden sticks. They were about two feet long, and some of them appeared to be pointy. And lying next to the sticks was a large hammer.

Miss Meely began to close the door. "If that's all you have on your minds, I'll say good-bye."

"Okay," Dottie said politely. "Good—"

The front door slammed shut.

"Did you see them?" Lee asked as they ran toward Shockly Manor. "Did you see the wooden sticks and the hammer?"

"No," said Dottie. "But did you notice how she looked? Different than the last time."

"Yeah, I noticed," Lee replied. "So?"

Dottie ignored his question. "And did you notice that funny smell?" she asked. The kids stopped only a few feet from the gates of the manor.

"What funny smell?" said T.J., stepping out from behind a nearby elm tree.

"Don't do that!" Lee yelled.

"Sorry," said T.J. "Now, what funny smell?"

Dottie twisted a lock of her curly red hair around her finger. "I don't know," she said. "It was kind of—um, fishy smelling."

"Look," Lee said nervously, "we'll fill you in at home. Right now, let's get out of here."

"We still have to walk those dogs around here," Dottie reminded him.

"Fine," Lee replied. "But we'll walk them in the opposite direction. Now let's go."

When the kids arrived home, they found Jimmy and Jay in the kitchen with Mrs. Klink. The three of them were trying to hide one of Phil's presents.

"I just don't know where to put it so he won't find it," said Mrs. Klink. She was standing next to the dishwasher.

"What is it?" asked T.J.

"It's a sweater, and I'm sure he'll—"

Just then, they heard a noise.

"What was that?" Lee looked up.

"It sounded like a car door," Jay replied.

"Oh, no," Mrs. Klink gasped. "Phil's back from the station house. We've got to hide this before he comes inside."

Quickly, Jimmy grabbed the brightly-wrapped box and threw it into the dishwasher. He slammed the door just as the Chief walked into the kitchen.

"Hi," he said, looking at all the smiling faces. "Why is everyone standing around here?"

"No reason, dear," Mrs. Klink replied. "We were just, uh, thinking about what we wanted for dinner."

The Chief walked over to Mrs. Klink and kissed her on the cheek. "Don't worry about fixing dinner tonight," he said. "I'm taking us all out to eat."

"You don't have to do that, dear," said

Mrs. Klink. She tried to move away from the dishwasher.

"I know," the Chief said with a smile. "It's just a way of thanking you for that great meal last night."

Mrs. Klink smiled back. "Oh, that was nothing. I—"

"Sure it was," said Phil Klink. He ushered everyone toward the kitchen door. "Now go get changed."

"We'd better do what he says," Jimmy whispered to Mrs. Klink. "He might get suspicious."

Mrs. Klink nodded. "All right, dear," she said as they walked out the doorway. "What are you going to do?"

"I'm going to the garage," the Chief called out. "Just as soon as I turn on the dishwasher. It's still full of last night's dishes."

Mrs. Klink and the kids turned toward the kitchen just as they heard the fatal *click, splosh.*

Everyone stared at Jimmy.

"Well," he said sheepishly. "I sure hope it's wash and wear."

When the family came home from dinner, Phil went into the den and Mrs. Klink made a beeline for the dishwasher. The kids went to T.J.'s room.

After going over all their information, the kids came up with one conclusion.

"We don't know a thing," Jay complained.

"Sure we do," said T.J. "We know that something weird is going on at the manor."

"And we know that two men bought the place for some weird club," said Dottie.

57

Jimmy leaned back against T.J.'s drawing table. "Maybe they're spies," he said.

"Spies!" Lee exclaimed.

"Yeah," Jimmy replied. "Old Man Shockly was an inventor. Maybe they're looking for some secret invention of his."

Lee began pacing back and forth. "Look, you guys," he said. "We've got a ghost that glows and gives warnings. We've got a lady who looks like a wolf and keeps sharp sticks and hammers. Then there are these two guys who dress in black, ride in a hearse—"

"It's a limousine," Jimmy corrected him.

Lee threw up his hands. "Well, it *looks* like a hearse! And these guys visit cemeteries." He looked around the room. "Don't you know what that means?"

"No, wise guy," Jimmy teased. "What does it mean?"

Lee moved close to the others. "It means ghosts aren't the only things that live in Shockly Manor. Pretty soon it's going to be—*vampires.*"

Dottie left the room. But for once she wasn't disgusted—she was scared.

She made her way down to the living room where Mr. and Mrs. Klink were watching television.

Dottie stood in the doorway.

Mrs. Klink looked up from the set. "What is it, sweetheart?"

"Aren't you feeling well?" asked the Chief.

Dottie's eyes filled with tears. "I want to go to bed. Could you tuck me in—please?"

Phil and Patty Klink put Dottie to bed. And

for half an hour they tried to convince her that there were no such things as ghosts.

"I don't know what stories you've been hearing," said Mrs. Klink. "But there's nothing to be afraid of. I promise you."

The Chief took Benny Boo from his shelf, and handed the bear to Dottie. "Sweetheart, I know how it was for you in the shelter. But it's different now. The Shadow Things are gone. And we're here to stay."

"You promise?" Dottie said softly.

"We promise," said Mrs. Klink.

Phil and Patty tucked Dottie in and kissed her good night.

That night, the house was quiet.

Outside, clouds glided in front of the moon, casting images like shadowy figures moving through the night.

But one figure was more than a shadow.

It glided noiselessly across the Klinks' backyard. It disappeared behind a tall oak tree near the back of the house. That tree's limbs stretched like tentacles toward the house.

The figure seem to float up the trunk of the tree, then along its thickest limb. Finally it stopped outside a window—Dottie's window.

Inside, Dottie slept fitfully, unaware that something had just arrived.

C·H·A·P·T·E·R
7

*P*owerful hands reached for the window.

Slowly they began pushing against the sash, straining to get it open.

But the old window was stuck, another thing Phil Klink had to fix—eventually.

The night caller braced itself on the branch and gave one more push. This time something gave— the tree limb. There was a loud crack, a yowl, and finally a solid thump as something hit the ground.

Dottie, frightened by the noises, woke up screaming.

Within seconds, her room was filled with people.

Mr. and Mrs. Klink arrived carrying flashlights. The boys arrived carrying anything they could find—baseball bats, hockey sticks, and a leaky water gun.

It took the Klinks several minutes to calm everybody down.

"Now what happened?" Phil Klink asked.

"I heard a noise outside my window," said Dottie. She jumped from her bed and ran to the window. "Someone was trying to break in."

"Are you sure about that?" asked Jay.

"You'd better believe it!" Dottie insisted.

T.J. took a deep breath. "Wow! Whoever it was left a real funky odor behind. Maybe Snoop can trail them."

Jimmy groaned. "Snoop's a basset hound, not a bloodhound."

"Come on," Jay said to Lee. "Let's get our equipment."

While Phil Klink pried open the window, Jay and Lee ran back to their rooms. When they returned, Jay had his flash camera and Lee carried his fingerprinting set.

"It's too dark out there," said Phil Klink, pulling his head in from the window. "I can't see the ground clearly."

"Let me try," said T.J. He leaned out the window and pointed his flashlight at the ground below. "There's a broken tree branch lying on the ground." T.J. swept his beam of light across the large oak's trunk. "And I can see where it broke off."

He stuck his head back into the room. "That branch used to reach this side of the house. I know, because I used to sneak out when—oops."

Phil and Patty gave him a hard look.

"We'll discuss that later," said the Chief.

"Why don't you dust for fingerprints, Lee?" Jay asked.

"All right," said Lee as he moved toward the window. "But don't expect me to find anything. Ghosts don't leave fingerprints."

"Ghosts don't break branches, either," said T.J. He took another deep breath as Lee passed him. "There's that smell again."

"I smell it, too," said Dottie.

Lee lowered his head and started removing his equipment.

"Why would the ghost from Shockly Manor come here?" Jay asked.

Lee was very upset. "Because we're marked," he exclaimed. He tried to open his bottle of fingerprinting dust, but the cap wouldn't come off. "Just like Mr. Landis said." He continued to pull. "And any minute, the Wolf Lady or the vampires are going to break in here, and then—it's sore throats for everybody!" Lee gave one final tug.

The cap came off, and the powder came out—all over T.J.

T.J. looked at the dark stains covering the front of his pajamas.

"I guess it wouldn't help to say I'm sorry?" Lee asked sheepishly.

T.J. shook his head. "Not a whole lot."

"Well, it doesn't matter," Lee shouted. "They're coming to get us, anyway!"

"Who are *they*?" Phil Klink demanded.

"And what is this nonsense about ghosts and vampires?" said Mrs. Klink.

"Nothing much," said Jimmy.

Phil walked over to Jimmy and looked him in the eye. "Well, *nothing much* could get you grounded for a month. Now what's going on?"

"We'd better tell them," Dottie said nervously. "Maybe they can help."

"I guess you're right," Jay agreed.

"It all started with the dogs," Lee blurted out. "We were walking them to get money to—"

"Buy detective stuff!" Dottie interrupted. She

still didn't want the Chief to find out about his surprise party.

"That's right," Jay said, catching on. "You see, Lee was walking by Shockly Manor . . ."

For the next fifteen minutes the kids tried to explain everything that had happened to them.

But the more they talked, the wilder it sounded. By the time they'd finished, even they weren't sure they believed it.

"I know it sounds nuts," T.J. pleaded. "But you've got to believe us. Dozerville is being invaded by monsters!"

Phil and Patty Klink looked at each other. *Here we go again*, they thought.

"Kids," said the Chief, rubbing his forehead. "I know you *think* you're tracking ghosts and goblins—"

"Vampires," Lee corrected.

Phil Klink smiled. "Uh, yes. Anyway, there's really a simple answer for all of this."

"Like what?" asked Lee.

"For one," said Mrs. Klink, "everyone knows about Tom Shockly's promise to return from the beyond. It's like an old folktale. But nobody really believes it."

"That's right," said the Chief. "Tom was, uh, eccentric."

"You mean wacko?" Jimmy asked.

The Chief frowned. "No, I mean eccentric. He was a great inventor, but a little—different."

"And," Mrs. Klink continued, "Elsa Meely is a rather unsociable person, but she's no Wolf Lady."

"But Mr. Landis said there might be ghosts in

that house," said T.J. "That's why he's glad to be selling it."

"P. T. Landis would be happy to sell *any* house in Creston Hills," said the Chief. He folded his hands across his chest. "Business has been pretty bad for him."

"Why?" asked Jimmy. He was feverishly trying to write everything down.

"Because no one ever sells their home in Creston Hills," Mrs. Klink replied. "They love it there. Mr. Landis hasn't sold any property in almost a year."

Lee seemed really confused. "Then what about Mr. Casper and Mr. Coombs? Why are they buying that creepy old house?"

The Chief shrugged his shoulders. "I have no idea," he said. "Probably for the very reasons they stated. But whatever the reasons are—they have nothing to do with ghosts."

"Want to bet?" said Lee as he started to clean off the windowsill.

"Look," T.J. said anxiously. "*Something* broke that branch off."

"It could have been the storm," said Mrs. Klink.

"And it could have been because someone was standing on it," said Jay. "That means some-one *was* trying to get in here!"

Phil Klink's eyes narrowed. "I think I'll check it out," he said, and left the room.

"Well, all of us could use a good night's sleep." Patty Klink lowered her voice. "Burglar or not, tomorrow is Phil's birthday party. And I expect us all to be alert and full of fun."

"Okay, then," said Jimmy. "Let's go, guys."

Jimmy turned to see Lee still bent over the windowsill. "Hey, are you coming?"

When Lee looked up, there was a funny expression on his face. "Huh?" he said. "Uh, sure. I'm coming."

"And leave the window open for a while," said T.J. "It really smells in here."

"It smells a little like garlic," said Mrs. Klink, sniffing the air.

Lee grabbed his things and headed toward the door. "Get some sleep, Dottie," he said. "And don't worry about a thing. We'll watch over you."

Lee reached out, mussed Dottie's hair, then left.

But once he was in the hallway, Lee's cheerfulness vanished. "It was no ghost that came up to Dottie's window," he said. "We had a real, live visitor."

"How do you know?" asked Jimmy.

Lee held up a piece of his fingerprinting tape. "Because I found some prints. They're too big for any of us, or Mrs. Klink. And I know what the Chief's look like." Lee slipped the tape into its special holder. "And ghosts don't leave prints."

Jay looked very serious as he and the boys started for their rooms. "Let's talk about this tomorrow morning," he said. "And guys—stay alert tonight."

With that, the boys went back to bed.

Just before he entered his room, T.J. called out, "Now it smells like garlic out here."

Lee's door slammed shut.

It was Saturday morning, Halloween. Breakfast was fast and a little gloomy.

Mrs. Klink had left early. She had some secret party errands to run. Dottie was still shaken from last night, and the Chief was annoyed by the morning headlines. The Creston Hills burglar had struck again.

"That does it," Phil Klink grumbled. "I'm going down to the station and see what I can do. This thief has got to be stopped." He rose from the table and grabbed his coat. "For all we know, he could have been the one outside Dottie's room."

"Then it wasn't the storm that broke that branch?" Jimmy asked with excitement.

"I doubt it," the Chief said seriously. A minute later, he was gone.

"That does it," said Jay angrily. "Something's going on at that manor. And now it's coming after us." He threw his napkin on the table. "Well, I say it's time we really found out what's what."

"How?" asked T.J.

"Ghost or no ghost," said Jay. "I'm going back to Shockly Manor tonight."

"I'll go with you," Jimmy volunteered.

T.J. swallowed hard. "So will I," he said.

"Me, too," said Dottie.

"You don't have to," Jay told her gently.

"Yes, I do," Dottie replied. "I don't know if it's a ghost or not. But I've got to find out."

There was a moment of silence, then Lee spoke up. "Count me in," he said.

"Are you sure about that, Lee?" Jay asked.

"You bet," said Lee, clearing his throat. "Whatever it was, it came after my little sister. And it's not going to get away with that."

"All right, then," Jay cheered. "Tonight, the Clues Kids go—ghost-busting!"

68

C·H·A·P·T·E·R
8

"*I*f we're going after a ghost," said T.J., "shouldn't we have *things*? Weapons or something?"

"You can't hurt a ghost," said Lee.

Jay started stacking the breakfast dishes in the sink. "Maybe we can't hurt it, but we can take pictures of it."

"Yeah," said Jimmy, rubbing his hands together. "And we can make tape recordings of its voice—or whatever sounds it makes."

"Maybe we could take along some rope," said Dottie. "Or a pair of the Chief's old handcuffs."

Jimmy wrinkled his brow. "Why?"

"Just in case it isn't a ghost." Dottie crossed her fingers. "And I hope it isn't."

"She's right," Jay agreed. "If it's solid, we can catch it."

"What if it's a solid vampire?" Lee asked.

"Uh, we could—" Jay stood scratching his head for a moment. Then his eyes widened. "*Cosmic Cop*! We never watched the last two episodes!"

"That's right," T.J. exclaimed. "We were so

busy Thursday and Friday, we forgot to watch the tapes."

"So let's see how he handled Telstar Toombs," Jay said enthusiastically. "Then we'll know what to bring for tonight."

"Tonight!" said Dottie, smacking her forehead. "Tonight is the Chief's surprise party!"

"That's right." Jimmy fell back against the wall. "How are we going to sneak out?"

"Who cares about that?" Dottie said angrily. "We didn't buy him a present yet."

"Okay, don't panic," said Jay. "How much money do we have?"

Dottie jumped down from her chair and ran over to one of the cabinets. She took out a box of instant soup mix, and removed one of the packets. The envelope had already been torn open. Dottie reached in and pulled out several dollar bills and some change.

"Nineteen dollars and sixty-four cents," she said, stuffing the money into her pocket.

"So that's where you hid it," said Lee.

"You would have spent it on something dumb if you knew where it was." Dottie put her hands on her hips.

"How'd you know we wouldn't find it?" asked Jimmy.

Dottie showed him the envelope. "None of us likes cream of asparagus soup."

The boys gagged.

"Come on," said Jay. "We'll go watch *Cosmic*, then go shopping for the Chief's present."

"And for our equipment for tonight," Jimmy added.

"We'd better bring everything we can find,"

T.J. said nervously. "Don't forget, tonight is Halloween."

The kids looked at each other. They knew they'd picked the worst night to go challenge the unknown.

Then again—who'd ever heard of a good night to go challenge the unknown?

Shrugging their shoulders, the kids headed for the living room.

All but Lee, that is. He rose from the table and hurried to the refrigerator.

"I'm going to be ready for anything tonight," he mumbled to himself. He opened the refrigerator and began digging around the bottom shelf.

And as scenes from *Revenge of the Vampire Fruit Bat* filled his head, Lee began stuffing bulbs of garlic into his pockets.

By late afternoon, the kids were roaming the town's shopping district—all five blocks of it. And they weren't all that happy. The last two episodes of *Cosmic Cop* hadn't been much help. Cosmic had destroyed Telstar by using pink lemonade. It had been a great scene, but none of the kids wanted to carry pink lemonade to Shockly Manor.

And they were discouraged for another reason.

"I don't believe it." Dottie sighed. "We still haven't found anything for the Chief."

"Don't worry," said Jay. "We'll find something soon. Just wait."

Jay was right. At the corner of Vincent and Price, the kids *did* find something. But it wasn't a present.

"Look," said T.J., pointing up the block. "Isn't that Miss Meely coming out of the supermarket?"

A few feet away, Lee's Wolf Lady was struggling with two large grocery bags as she headed
for her car.

"Come on," Jay said quickly. "Let's see what
she's up to."

"Can we help you?" Jimmy offered as they
reached Miss Meely's car.

She peeked over her packages and frowned.
"No, thank you, I—"

"I'll get that for you," said T.J., opening the
car door.

"And I'll get this." Jimmy tried to take one of
the packages.

Suddenly he stopped. Across the top of the
bags, Miss Meely locked eyes with him. "I don't
need your help, thank you," she said through
clenched teeth.

She shoved the bags into her car and slammed
the door.

"You children seem unavoidable," she said.

"We're trustworthy and likable, though." Jay
flashed a big smile at her.

"I wonder," she said, as she stepped into her
car. "I wonder."

Just before Miss Meely closed the door, Dottie
managed to look inside one of the bags. It seemed
to be filled with a lot of small cans. But before
Dottie could get closer, Miss Meely drove away.

"Well, that was a waste of time," said Jay.
"Let's go get some film and audio tapes. We're
going to—"

"Look," said T.J. This time he was pointing
to a car cruising by—a long, black limousine.

"Casper and Coombs," said Lee. He spoke in
a low voice, as if he were afraid they'd hear

him. "The sun starts to go down—and they come out."

The kids watched the sleek vehicle move slowly and silently up the street.

"What do you think they're looking for?" T.J. asked.

"Dinner," said Lee, clutching at the garlic in his pocket.

"Well, hello there," someone called from behind them.

The kids turned to find Mr. Landis standing in the doorway of a travel agency.

"I keep running into you kids," he said.

"Everyone says that about us," said Jay, as he led the kids over.

"Are you going on a trip?" asked Dottie.

"Yes, I am," Mr. Landis replied cheerfully. "A vacation. I leave Tuesday morning, and the sale of Shockly Manor made it all possible."

"Ghost and all," Lee mumbled.

"Ghost and all," Mr. Landis repeated. "That reminds me," he said, leaning closer to them. "About that earring you found—"

Dottie glanced at Jimmy.

"Yeah," said Jimmy. "I told him."

"Anyway," Mr. Landis continued, "I really think you should drop it by my office. It might belong to someone who came to see the house. And a pearl set in gold is a very valuable piece."

"You're right, sir," said Jay. "We'll drop it off on Monday, right after school."

Mr. Landis patted Jay on the shoulder. "That's fine. Now I have to run along. Have fun trick-or-treating tonight," he said.

The kids watched as he limped away.

"Boy," Jay exclaimed. "Everybody's out today. Miss Meely, Casper and Coombs, even Mr. Landis."

"I'll be sorry to give it back," said Dottie. "But I guess it's the right thing to do."

"Sure it is," said Jay. "Now let's go find the Chief's present."

Phil Klink's surprise party started with a bang. The Chief blew a tire coming into the driveway.

But after that, it was fun, fun, fun.

For the first half hour, the kids were everywhere. They helped serve food, hang up coats, and clean up spills.

But by seven-thirty, they were ready to go on their mission. And T.J. had designed their gear.

Jimmy and Jay were spacemen. Lee was disguised as a scarecrow. T.J. wore a homemade pirate's costume, complete with bushy red moustache. And Dottie looked lovely as a ladybug. She even had a red football helmet with fake antennae.

"Where will you be?" Mrs. Klink asked them as they headed for the back door.

"We'll be trick-or-treating in the neighborhood," said Jimmy anxiously. "With a few—friends."

"Well, don't stay out too long," Mrs. Klink replied. "There'll be plenty of food and goodies waiting for you right here."

"Okay," said Jimmy.

"And one more thing." Mrs. Klink walked over to them. "Don't feel badly that you couldn't find a gift. Phil loves you, no matter what." She smiled and ushered them out the door. "Now go have a good time."

"We made it," said Jimmy once they were pedaling through town.

"Yeah," said Lee. "But I sure feel cheap, tricking Mrs. Klink like that."

"So do I," said Jay. "But it's for a good cause. Let's ride."

It was definitely Halloween night. The wind howled through the trees and along the streets. The moon was a big yellow ball in a blue-black sky. And everywhere pint-sized ghosts, ghouls, and witches roamed the streets. They crept up on their victims' houses and robbed them of their valuables—apples, jelly beans, and chocolate bars. No adult was safe.

It took only a few minutes for the kids to reach Shockly Manor. They rode past it, then stopped just down the street.

"We'll hide our bikes in these bushes," said Jay. "Then we'll take our positions. Do you guys remember where you're supposed to be?"

"Home," said Lee. There was a faint tremor in his voice.

"Very funny." Jimmy gave him a look. "Now, let's go."

Swiftly and quietly the kids made their way through the gates of the manor.

Once they were on the grounds, they split into two groups. Jimmy and Lee took the right side, Jay, T.J., and Dottie took the left.

"You remember what to do if we see anything?" asked Jimmy. The two boys had reached their position among the bushes.

Lee felt as if something were watching him. "Yeah," he replied. "A lot of screaming."

Jimmy groaned.

———•———

On the other side of the house, Jay and *his* team lay hidden under the tall hedges.

"Do you think we'll see anything?" Dottie asked.

"Unfortunately—yes," T.J. replied.

It was a long wait for both teams. And for a while it looked as if nothing was going to happen. But just as they were about to give up, that changed.

Jimmy and Lee spotted a dark-clad figure creeping out from the bushes, only a few feet away from them.

The figure appeared to be carrying a small parcel as it stumbled to the side of the house.

Then, with a clumsy effort, the figure climbed through a first-floor window and was swallowed by the darkness inside.

"Hey," Lee whispered, "vampires aren't that clumsy."

"You're right," said Jimmy as he rose to his feet. "That guy walked like he had a twisted ankle or something. Come on, let's see what he's up to."

The two boys darted from their hiding place, climbed through the window, and disappeared inside.

At almost that very instant, Jay's team also spotted something.

Someone stepped forward from the hedges and hurried over to the kitchen entrance.

The kids heard a jingling sound. Then the door opened and the figure disappeared inside.

"Do you think it was Mr. Casper or Mr. Coombs?" asked T.J.

"No," Jay replied. "That person was too short."

"I think he was carrying something," said Dottie.

"Let's find out what." Followed by the others, Jay slipped from his hiding place and hurried toward the house.

When they got inside, the first thing the Clues Kids saw was the door to the cellar. Jay took hold of the handle and pulled. With amazing ease, the door swung open.

"These hinges have been oiled," Jay whispered. "Someone's been using this door a lot."

Carefully the three went down the stone steps into the damp, cold basement.

Once inside, Dottie turned on a small flashlight.

Pressing close together, the kids followed a long, narrow passage that led through a maze of old furniture and household equipment.

At the end of the passage was a small room with a light on. Someone was in there. Someone—or something.

Through the almost smothering quiet of the basement, the kids could hear a sound. A strange, sinister sound—like the hissing of a giant snake.

C·H·A·P·T·E·R
9

"*I*t's a *giant snake*," T.J. said in a low, raspy voice. "We didn't come prepared to take on a giant snake."

Jay quickly put his finger to his lips. "Keep it down," he whispered. "I don't know what it is, but it doesn't sound like a snake."

"It doesn't sound like a breakfast cereal, either," T.J. argued. "I say we go get a little help."

"Like who?"

"I hear the Marines are pretty tough," T.J. replied.

"You want everybody laughing at us again?" Jay said. "We've got to find out what's going on first. Now you, Dottie, and I will—" Jay stopped.

He turned to where Dottie had been standing. She was gone.

Without hesitation, the two boys crept forward and peeked into the room.

At first, all they saw were damp stone walls and more piles of boxes and stuff. Then T.J. spotted Dottie crouched down behind a large packing crate.

What are you doing? Jay gestured once they had reached her hiding place.

Dottie pointed to the front of the room. She signaled that the hissing noise was coming from there.

The three children peeked over the crate, and were shocked at what they saw. At the front of the room was a laboratory table, complete with test tubes, bottles of fluid, and strange electrical equipment.

The light in the room came from a single bulb hanging over the table. Under that bulb stood a hunched figure. The kids couldn't see him clearly, but he seemed to be working on something in a large, wicker basket.

"Oh, great!" T.J. muttered. "Now we're up against Dr. Frankenstein, too."

Carefully, Jay pulled his camera from his costume. He signaled the others, and slowly, cautiously, they began to sneak closer to the table.

All we need is one good picture, Jay thought to himself. *Then people will believe us.*

They were only a few feet from the table now. One more step, and they'd be in position to take the picture—and run.

Unfortunately, Jay took that next step—right into a stack of metal pipes. And the pipes fell to the stone floor with a deafening crash.

Screams of panic echoed off the walls, and the hunched figure whirled around, holding something over its head.

Instantly, T.J. jumped between the figure and the kids. "Run, you guys," he shouted, waving his sword in the air. "I'll draw and quarter-pound this knave!" He pronounced the K, which is usually silent.

But suddenly—everyone recognized each

other. And the only thing missing was dramatic music.

"Miss Meely!" the kids shouted.

"You!" Miss Meely exclaimed.

The crabby lady stood before the children, wearing jeans and an oversize sweater. She held a hammer in one hand, and a wooden slat in the other.

"What are you children doing here?" she gasped.

"Catching a ghost—we thought," said T.J.

"A ghost?" Miss Meely almost smiled. She took a couple of deep breaths, stepped backwards, and slumped down on a dusty stool.

That was when the kids got a good look at what she had been doing.

A crude box sat on the table. It was made from wooden slats, and padded with lots of old cloth.

The wicker basket sat next to the box, and in it was a mother cat and her kittens.

Dottie's eyes sparkled, growing wide with amazement. She stared at the cat, with its big brown eyes and soft black-and-white fur. "*This* is what you've been doing around here!" she said.

"I'm afraid so," said Miss Meely, still trying to catch her breath.

T.J. tilted his buccaneer hat back on his head. "You mean," he said, "this is why you've been creeping around—"

"Creeping!" Miss Meely's back stiffened, and some of her crankiness came back. "I'll have you know I have a key to this house."

"Because you and Mr. Shockly were friends,"

said Dottie. "And you've been coming here to take care of this cat and her kittens." She moved closer to the basket.

"Careful," Miss Meely warned. "The mother doesn't like anyone to get too close, even me."

"A cat," said T.J., snapping his fingers. "That's what was making that hissing sound! Boy, do I feel dumb."

"You should," Dottie teased. She turned toward Miss Meely. "Why have you kept it a secret?"

Miss Meely placed the wooden slat on the floor. "I was afraid old money-hungry P.T. Landis would find them and throw them out on the street." She sighed. "He wouldn't want anything in here that would spoil his chance of selling the place."

"And that's why you kept chasing us away," said Jay. "You were afraid we'd find the cats."

"What cats?"

Everyone turned to see Jimmy and Lee entering the room.

"What cats are you guys talking about?" Jimmy repeated.

Dottie pointed to the basket. "These cats."

While Jimmy and Lee peeked into the basket, the other kids told them the story.

"Wow," said Jimmy, pointing to the kittens. "One black, one white, and three mixed. I wish we could have one."

"Cats," Lee exclaimed. "That's why the dogs went crazy." He slapped his hand to his forehead. "They could smell the cats."

"Well, that's the story," said Jimmy, throwing up his hands. "No ghosts, no vampires. Just a nice lady doing a good deed. Guess we can go home now."

Dottie reached into her pocket. "If you've been sneaking in and out of the house," she said, "then this must be yours. I found it upstairs." Dottie held out the pearl earring.

Instantly, Miss Meely's eyes narrowed. "That's mine, all right," she said. She took the earring and examined it. "But I didn't lose it here. It was *stolen* two days ago, when my house was robbed."

"By the Creston Hills burglar?" asked Jimmy.

"Most likely," Miss Meely replied bitterly. "Whoever it was, he came and went like a phantom. And took most of my jewelry with him."

"Then the thief must have come in here," said Jimmy.

"What for?" asked Dottie. "To hide from someone?"

Jay stood scratching his head for a minute. Then his eyes widened, and his mouth dropped open.

"Not to hide himself—" he shouted. "To hide the loot!"

"Yeah," said Jimmy. "What better place to hide stuff than in a haunted house?"

Lee shook his head. "Especially if the crook knew the house wasn't haunted."

"*Especially* if you knew the house real well," said Jay.

"The Chief said the burglar seems to know this neighborhood," Dottie added.

Lee began pacing the floor. "But how would he know someone wouldn't find the stuff here?"

"Or that the house wouldn't be sold?" Miss Meely added, getting caught up in the mystery.

Again, the room was silent. Everyone thought and thought, trying to solve the crooked problem. Then, once again, a light went on in Jay's head.

"Because he'd be the first one to know if the house was sold!" Jay exclaimed.

"Oh, boy!" said Jimmy, realizing what his brother was getting at. "The burglar is someone who knows the home and the neighborhood."

Jay tensed with excitement. "He can get in and out of any house in the area without breaking a lock or window—"

"Because he has the keys!" Dottie exclaimed.

"Wait a minute!" Lee looked scared. "How did you guys get in here?"

"We followed Miss Meely into the cellar," T.J. replied.

"Jimmy and I followed someone inside, too," said Lee.

Jimmy looked around the room. "He's right. We followed a man in black. He came in through the side window."

"If you followed her," Lee said, pointing at Miss Meely, "who did we follow?"

The sound of creaking hinges caused everyone to turn toward the door. There stood Mr. P.T. Landis, dressed in black and holding a small black satchel.

"Evening, all," he said as a wicked smile crossed his face. "I must congratulate you *children* on some very good sleuthing." He took two steps into the room.

"You're limping," Jay said sarcastically. "Hurt yourself climbing a tree?"

"You mean he was the guy outside Dottie's window?" yelled Lee.

"That's right," admitted Mr. Landis. "I've been robbing the houses in Creston Hills. And I've been stashing my loot here at Shockly Manor." Mr. Landis took a step back. "However, by Tuesday evening, I'll be in South America."

"Not after we tell the police about you!" shouted Jimmy.

Lee glared at him. "Why'd you have to say that? You know what he's going to say now, don't you?"

"I'm afraid I can't let you get to the police," Mr. Landis said calmly. "That would spoil my vacation. So—"

With amazing speed, Mr. Landis suddenly ducked out the door and slammed it shut. The next second the kids heard a strange humming sound—then a loud click.

Everyone ran to the door and tried to push it open. But it was no good. The solid metal door wouldn't budge.

"Great thing, these electromagnetic locks," Mr. Landis yelled through the door. "Mr. Shockly wanted to be sure no one could get into his laboratory." There was a brief moment of silence. Then he added, "Of course —no one can get out, either."

Desperately, the kids and Miss Meely began looking around the room. But there were no windows, and no other doors.

They were trapped!

C·H·A·P·T·E·R
10

"*D*on't panic," said Jimmy. "Just keep saying, 'Everything is *fine*.' "

T.J. grabbed Jimmy by his retro rockets and spun him around. "Look, we're trapped in a basement, in a locked room, in an empty house. And the only guy who knows we're here is the guy who trapped us."

T.J. leaned close to Jimmy. "That is not *fine*!" he shouted.

"It's not my fault we're in this mess!" yelled Jimmy. "Who's the one—"

"Knock it off, you guys," said Jay. "We've got to get out of here and stop Mr. Landis."

"Yes," Miss Meely agreed. "He's about to escape with all my jewelry."

Jimmy and T.J. calmed down.

"Okay, everybody," said Lee. "We've got to think. How do we get past an electromagnetic lock?"

For the next few minutes, things looked hopeless. The kids and Miss Meely searched the room once again. They checked the walls, the floors, and the ceiling, hoping to find a switch for the door, or another way out.

But the end result was—nothing.

Then, an idea for escape appeared. Jay was sitting on the laboratory table when it hit him.

"Owww," he said.

"What's wrong?" asked Dottie.

"I leaned back, and banged my head against this stupid equipment," Jay replied, rubbing his head.

"I wonder what he used all that electrical stuff for," said T.J.

"Probably for his inventions and—" Suddenly Jay let out a terrific cheer. "Cosmic Cop!"

Lee frowned at him. "I don't think Cosmic is going to hear you, Jay," he said.

Jay leaped off the table. "No, you don't get it. Remember how Cosmic Cop stopped Telstar Toombs?"

"With pink lemonade," said T.J.

Jay groaned. "No, he used the pink lemonade to *short-circuit* him."

"I get it," said Jimmy. "You mean we could short-circuit the door?"

"Sure. It's powered by electricity. If we can overload it—we're out of here!"

"Sure, I remember that from school," said Jimmy. "But what do we use?"

"I suggest *this*," Miss Meely said cheerfully. She pointed to a box-shaped piece of machinery sitting on the floor. "That contraption is a small generator. Thomas built it just in case there was ever a power failure."

Jay ran over to the generator. "Great," he said. "I saw some coils of wire in that corner. And I'll need some wire cutters, and some heavy-duty tape."

"I'll get the wire," said T.J.

Dottie started running toward the back of the room. "I saw some tape on a box back here!" she cried.

"There are some wire cutters up here." Lee reached across the top of the worktable. "Here."

In a few seconds the kids had gathered all their equipment and joined Jay around the generator.

"What are you going to do now?" asked Dottie.

Jay began stripping the wire and attaching it to the generator. "We've got to run the wires from the generator to the magnetic plate over the lock."

"Are you sure about that?" asked T.J., adjusting his moustache.

"No," Jay said flatly.

T.J. smiled. "Okay. Just checking."

"Just to be safe," said Miss Meely, "I'll be the one to turn on the power."

"That's okay with me," Jay replied.

Miss Meely sighed. "I was afraid you'd say that."

Moving quickly, Jay attached the wires to the power source. Then he taped the other ends to the door.

"It's all set," he said finally. "Whenever you're ready, Miss Meely."

Miss Meely placed one hand on the generator switch, and the other over her eyes. "Here goes!"

She threw the switch, and the motor began to whine.

"The generator works," Lee cheered.

Suddenly there was a flash of light, and then

a loud, crackling sound. The bulb blew out, the mother cat hissed, and Miss Meely screamed.

Then, all was quiet. The smell of burning wires filled the room.

A nervous smile appeared on Jay's face. "That was supposed to happen . . . I think."

"Can we try the door?" asked Jimmy.

"After we disconnect the wires," said Jay.

Dottie switched on her flashlight and aimed it at the generator. Miss Meely picked up a piece of wood and knocked the wires loose.

"Okay," said Jay. "Let's try it, when I say three."

Jay and the kids huddled together, ready to charge the door.

"One . . ." said Jay. "Two . . . three!"

The kids screamed and ran full-speed into their target.

The heavy metal door swung wide open, slamming into the wall behind it.

"We're free," T.J. cheered. "My shoulder's sore, but we're free."

Jimmy looked down at his costume. "I think I've damaged my retro rockets," he said. The little plastic tubes were smashed.

"No time for that now," Jay exclaimed. "We've got to get upstairs and stop Mr. Landis!"

The basement stairs led into the kitchen of Shockly Manor. Through the darkness, they could just see the old wooden cabinets and marble counter tops.

Using his flashlight, Jimmy led the way down a couple of corridors and out into the main hall.

Everything was exactly as they remembered

it—the high ceilings, the paintings on the walls, the large oriental rug on the floor.

Across the room to their right was the winding stairway to the next floor. Next to it was a small table. And the kids could just make out a door beneath the stairs.

"I'll check that out," said T.J., pointing to the door.

"I'll go with you," said Jimmy.

The two boys moved cautiously across the room, leaving the other kids and Miss Meely to keep watch.

The front door was to their left, and straight ahead was the corridor leading to the living room.

Dottie moved her flashlight all around. "Where do you think he is?" Her voice sounded a little angry.

"He could be anywhere in the house," Jay whispered. "Let's look around here first, then we'll try upstairs."

At the mention of stairs, Dottie aimed her beam at the top landing. And there he was.

"It's him," Dottie screamed. "It's Mr. Landis, and he's got the loot."

Miss Meely gasped. "Oh, my goodness!"

"Block the door!" Jay shouted. He, Miss Meely, and the other kids ran over and placed themselves between Mr. Landis and freedom.

"I can't seem to get rid of you kids," Mr. Landis shouted. "Well, I'm still leaving here with these jewels. And nothing is going to stop me!"

With that, Mr. Landis came racing down the stairs. The look in his eyes told the kids he intended to ram right through them.

Lee swallowed hard. "You think this is going to hurt?" he asked Jay.

"Yes," Jay replied, inching closer to the group. "But only for a little while."

Just then they saw T.J. leap onto the table by the stairs. He took his wooden sword and jammed it between the rungs of the railing and across the stairs.

"Take this, you scurvy knave." Again, T.J. pronounced the K.

Mr. Landis tripped over the sword and came tumbling down the stairs. His bag of loot went flying through the air, straight into Lee's waiting hands.

"The rug!" Dottie yelled.

Without hesitation all the kids grabbed one end of the large rug, flipped it over the stunned villain, and rolled him up, snug and tight.

When the job was done, Mr. Landis's head was the only thing sticking out.

Then everyone quickly sat down—hard—on the crook.

Dottie leaned over the struggling realtor's head and smiled. "Trick or treat, Mr. Landis."

"I'll go for help," said Miss Meely. She opened the door and was caught in a glare of bright lights.

Phil Klink, eight police officers, and a half dozen friends came storming through the door.

"Everybody freeze," the Chief shouted.

"I love it when he does that," said T.J.

"Wait a minute," said Jimmy. "How'd he know where we were?"

"I left him a note," said Dottie. She opened her arms as the Chief came over to hug her.

The other kids simply smiled and joined in.

It was ten o'clock by the time everyone returned to the Klinks' home. Phil, Patty, and all the people from the party gathered in the living room to hear the kids' story.

Naturally, Jimmy did most of the talking. But the others managed to get in a few details of their own.

"So that's when I remembered the drawings on Mr. Landis's wall," said Jay. He sat on the floor munching cheese snacks. "The Chief said that the crook knew all the houses real well. And Mr. Landis had diagrams of every house in Creston Hills."

"Yeah," said T.J. "And he got his limp when he fell from our tree."

"He wanted to steal back the earring Dottie found," Jimmy added. "And—"

"And," said Dottie. She moved closer to the Chief and Mrs. Klink. "We're . . . we're real sorry for worrying you and sneaking out to Shockly Manor."

The Chief gently placed his hand on Dottie's shoulder. "We'll all discuss this in the morning," he said.

"Was there something else you wanted to say?" Mrs. Klink asked gently.

Jay offered Phil Klink a large white envelope. "We're sorry that we couldn't get you a present," he said sadly.

T.J. pulled off his pirate moustache and hat. "Truth is, Chief, we didn't have enough money to buy you—something special."

"Special?" Phil asked.

"Yeah," Lee replied. "Something that would show you how we really feel about you."

Slowly Phil leaned forward. He looked at each of the kids, and a warm smile appeared on his face. "Kids, each of you is special to me," he said. "And together you're the greatest gift I could ever hope for."

"That goes for both of us," said Mrs. Klink. She wiped her eyes, and sniffled a bit. "Now, how about a hug?"

"No problem!" the kids cheered. Laughing and giggling, they piled all over the Klinks.

"This would make a terrific photo for the papers," said Tabby Lloyd. She was a friend of the family, and the best reporter on the *Dozerville Herald*, the town paper.

"You're right," said Phil Klink. "I'd love a good picture of you kids."

"And we could buy a great frame to put it in," Dottie said eagerly. "That would be a great present."

"Yes, it would." Phil hugged the kids closer.

"So everything worked out just fine," said Jimmy. "And we can close this case with a—"

"Wait a minute," Lee interrupted. "There's one thing that still bothers me." Lee walked to the center of the room. "What about Mr. Casper and Mr. Coombs?"

"Oh, I can tell you about them," said Patty Klink. "They're moving their business into Dozerville."

"What business?" asked Jimmy.

"They own a large florist shop. And they specialize in exotic flowers."

95

"But why would they go to a cemetery?" asked Jay.

Mrs. Klink chuckled. "Because they love a certain type of flower that grows at night," she said. "And Ravenswood has a special garden of night-growing flowers."

"So you see," said Jimmy, "it's like I said from the start. There are no ghosts."

Just then—from outside the house—a horrible howl ripped through the night.

Lee turned and headed for the kitchen.

"Where are you going?" asked Jimmy.

"To get more garlic," he said. "Sometimes, you just can't be too careful." Everybody in the room burst out laughing.

At last the people of Dozerville could close their doors to the children of Halloween. As they tucked themselves into bed for the night, they could rest easier. Because they knew that they were protected by an ever-vigilant team of clever, resourceful, and slightly bizarre children. The Clues Kids.